Malaika's Winter Carnival

PICTURES BY

Nadia L. Hohn   Irene Luxbacher

GROUNDWOOD BOOKS
HOUSE OF ANANSI PRESS
TORONTO BERKELEY

Groundwood Books / House of Anansi Press
groundwoodbooks.com

We acknowledge for their financial support of our publishing program
the Canada Council for the Arts, the Ontario Arts Council and the
Government of Canada.

 Canada Council **Conseil des Arts**
for the Arts **du Canada**

 ONTARIO ARTS COUNCIL
CONSEIL DES ARTS DE L'ONTARIO
an Ontario government agency
un organisme du gouvernement de l'Ontario

With the participation of the Government of Canada | Canadä
Avec la participation du gouvernement du Canada

Library and Archives Canada Cataloguing in Publication
Hohn, Nadia L., author
Malaika's winter carnival / Nadia L. Hohn ; pictures by Irene
Luxbacher.
Issued in print and electronic formats.
ISBN 978-1-55498-920-1 (hardcover).—ISBN 978-1-55498-921-8 (pdf)
I. Luxbacher, Irene, illustrator II. Title.
PS8615.O396M36 2017   jC813'.6   C2016-908196-6
                                        C2016-908197-4

The illustrations were done in mixed media, graphite and oils on paper.
Design by Michael Solomon
Printed and bound in Malaysia

 **MIX**
Paper from
responsible sources
FSC® C012700
FSC
www.fsc.org

For Mummy — NH

For my family …
… with many thanks to
Nadia Hohn and everyone at
Groundwood Books — IL

Bienvenue à Québec: Welcome to Quebec.
breadfruit: A starchy tropical fruit that can be
    roasted, fried, baked or boiled. Its texture
    and taste have been compared to fresh
    bread or potato.
chinep: A tropical fruit, also called genip or
    Spanish lime. It has a hard green skin on
    the outside and a fleshy inside like a grape.
enchanté: Pleased to meet you.
famille: Family.
mangeons: Let's eat.
toque: A warm, close-fitting knit hat.

"My girl, look at you. You almost as big as me," Mummy laugh. She press me into her flower dress with her soft belly and smell of cocoa butter beside my head. Grandma hug us too. I don't want to let go.

When I look up, I see a tall pale man smiling at me.

"Malaika, baby, this is Mr. Frédéric. Frédéric, this is my little Malaika," Mummy say.

"*Enchanté*, Malaika," he say, with a different talk than Mummy, and his hand stretch out to me.

I don't know what to do.

"Galang, chile. Shake he hand.
It's the custom," Grandma say,
patting my shoulder.

I put my small hand up to his big
hand, and he shake it.

"I'm Adèle," say a girl with the same different talk as
Mr. Frédéric. "We are going to become *famille*, sisters, soon."
She kiss me on two side of my face.

I am the flower girl at Mummy and
Mr. Frédéric's wedding. Grandma plait my
hair with flower and ribbon.
   "Smile, Malaika! You fit that dress so nice,"
say Ms. Chin, the tailor lady.

Everyone from our district come to the church to see Mummy marry the French Canadian with his red-hair little girl.

"Look," Adèle say, pointing to Mr. Frédéric kissing Mummy. I cover my eyes.

After, we go to the beach at Cutty's restaurant where sweet reggae music play. The Chinese lanterns glow, and the crickets call quiet ocean waves. Mummy and Mr. Frédéric look so happy.

I sit by myself.
Then Adèle come
pull me up to dance.
I don't want to
dance.

Every day, I help Grandma bake sweet bread, fry fish and make her special coconut drops. Grandma cook this food when someone leave our district.

One day, we visit the beach where I build castles
and bury Adèle in the sand. Then she run into the
sea to wash it all off. Then we do it all over again.

On the last day, Uncle Ewart throw a big cookout and all of my cousins and school friends come to see us off. Even my teacher come. I cry and cry.

"Malaika, I know dis won't be easy,
but I think you're going to like Canada,"
Mummy say as she hold me.

The next day, Uncle Ewart and cousin Fitzroy
pack a minibus to get ready to drive all of us to the
airport. But first I hug Grandma for a long time.
She wave at us from the house, holding her tissue.

When our airplane land, Mummy give me a big purple coat with fur on the hood to put on. I step outside, and my body feel cold all over. I see a white puff when I breathe out.

"*Bienvenue à Québec*, Malaika," Mr. Frédéric say.
"You will share your room with Adèle and have
your own bed," Mummy say.
"Like sisters," Adèle say. She smile a toothy grin.

The next day, I go to my new school. Mummy make me wear a long pants called long johns, two pair of wool socks, an undershirt, a turtleneck, a sweater and a coat. I have two pairs of mitts on and a hat them call "toque" and earmuffs. The boots are a little big, but Mr. Frédéric say they will last two winters.

When I get there, the children speak a different way. The teacher speak a different way. No one understand me. I hate it.

One day, Mummy and Mr. Frédéric take Adèle
and me to what they call carnival.
  Adèle pull my hand over to her snow castle
made with colorful cones — green and blue, red
and yellow. But I don't care.

"This is no carnival. I don't see no costumes. This is an ugly castle. I hate it," I scream.
I kick down the snow castle. I pick off the ice cones and throw them on the ground. They make a sound like breaking glass.
Adèle's face look like it break apart too.

The next morning, Mummy wake me up.

"There's someone who want to see you," she say.

She put the computer on my lap.

"Grandma!" I say.

"Malaika? Is that you?" she say, squinting her eye.

Seeing Grandma make me think about goats on the roadside and chinep and shiny black shoes at church. Think about warm breeze and roosters crowing in the morning and poinsettia flowers at Christmas time. Think about school uniform and roasted breadfruit with salt and all of my friends and cousins.

Grandma make me feel so happy again
that I reach out to hug her. But I can't.
We both cry when she have to go.

Out the window, I see Adèle pour red water
onto the snow, then pack the snow into cups. Then
green water, then blue water, then yellow…

I put on my coat, hat and all my things and run
outside. I take a deep breath.

"I'm sorry, Adèle."

She smile then give me a big hug.

We look up at the fat snowflakes fallin' from the sky.

"Malaika, *mangeons*!" Adèle say.

"What?" I say.

"Let's eat," she say. She open her mouth as the tiny
icy crystals land on her tongue. I do the same and gobble
each one. I smile, a big smile. Then I start to laugh and
she do too. I laugh with my sister until my belly hurt.